The Case of the Secret Valentine

by James Preller
illustrated by John Speirs
cover illustration by R. W. Alley

A
LITTLE APPLE
PAPERBACK

SCHOLASTIC INC.
New York Toronto London Auckland Sydney
Mexico City New Delhi Hong Kong

For Jen Goeke,
with thanks for inviting me into
her second grade classroom, as well as for providing
a bright, shining example of everything
a teacher should be;

and lastly, special thanks to the kids in Ms. Goeke's
1997–98 classroom: David, Erin, Abigail, Elizabeth, Dayna,
Cody, Ronald, Kelsey, Kathryn, Danica, Cecelia, Alexander,
Zachory, Kimberley, Amanda, Tristin, Samuel, Mandi,
Joshua, Corey, Michael, and Olivia!

ISBN 0-590-69127-9

12 11   1 2 3 4/0

Printed in the U.S.A.   40
First Scholastic printing, January 1999

CONTENTS

Chapter One

A Mysterious Valentine

My name is Jigsaw Jones.

I'm a detective. For a dollar a day, I make problems go away.

My real name is Theodore. But I don't exactly brag about it. All my friends call me Jigsaw. That's because I love doing jigsaw puzzles. And I love solving mysteries. I do both the same way: one piece at a time.

I have a partner. Her name is Mila. Together, we're the best detectives in the second grade. Then again, that's not saying

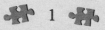 1

a whole lot. We're the *only* detectives in the second grade.

Well, that's not true. Not anymore. We *were* the only detectives in the second grade. But then Bobby Solofsky started his own detective business.

The copycat.

It all started on a Sunday like any other. I woke up. I messed around. Then Mila came over. I had to lock Rags, my big, lazy dog, in the kitchen. Mila is allergic to fur. But don't worry about Rags. He doesn't mind lying around the kitchen. All Rags does is eat and sleep and drool anyway. Well, sometimes he barks.

Mila and I were doing a special project. We had to draw a life-size picture of Abraham Lincoln. It was for extra credit. Our teacher, Ms. Gleason, said she'd hang it in the hall for Presidents' Day. We also had to write ten facts about Abraham Lincoln. So far, we had three:

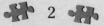

1. His nickname was Honest Abe.
2. He was the sixteenth president.
3. He was a good wrestler.

Mila smoothed out a long roll of brown paper across the living room floor. She picked up a ruler. Measuring was her job. Twelve inches make a foot. Abraham Lincoln was six feet, plus four more inches. Add that all up and you've got, well, Abraham Lincoln. That's without the big hat. I figure Abe would have been a good basketball player. I'm pretty sure he could have beaten George Washington in a game of H-O-R-S-E.

Then the doorbell rang.

"I'll get it, Mrs. Jones," Mila called out. She ran to open the front door. "Hmmm. That's funny. No one's here." Mila picked up something from the ground. She handed it to me. "I found this on the stoop."

I looked at the envelope. There was a

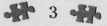

pink heart and T-H-E-O-D-O-O-R was written across the top. It was spelled wrong. There's no *door* in Theodore. But that wasn't the weird thing. Each letter was cut out from a magazine and pasted on.

There was a note inside. It was also in cutout letters. The note said:

TO THEODOOR
GUSS WHO?
YOUR SECRIT
ADMIRROR

My stomach jiggled. It felt like I had swallowed a bunch of Mexican jumping beans. My palms started to sweat. The Mexican jumping beans danced the macarena in my belly.

Mila read the note. "'G-U-S-S W-H-O?'" she asked. "What's that mean? Oh, I understand. It's spelled wrong. It's supposed to say 'Guess Who.'"

My mom came into the room. "Who was at the door?"

"Nobody," I explained.

"Jigsaw got a secret valentine!" Mila sang. She showed the note to my mom.

"'To Theodore,'" my mom read. "Isn't that lovely!"

Yeah, I thought to myself. Just lovely. About as lovely as getting drooled on by Rags. My mom smiled at me. A big, happy smile. Then she left the room, humming softly as she went.

"This is the worst thing that could ever

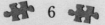

happen," I said to Mila. "Ever. In the whole world."

"I think it's cute," Mila said.

"Cute?" I complained. "Cute?! This isn't cute. This is rotten."

"No," Mila said. "This is a mystery."

Chapter Two
Clues and More Clues

Mila didn't waste any time on the school bus Monday morning. "Did you bring the valentine?" she asked.

"Stop calling it a valentine," I complained. "It's a clue."

Mila took the note from my hand and read it over again. She wasn't in a hurry.

"What do you think?" I asked.

"Well," Mila said, "she's not a very good speller." Mila pointed to the words

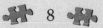

SECRIT
and
ADMIRROR
and
GUSS.

"Look," Mila said. "They are spelled wrong."

I took her word for it.

"But I'm wondering why she cut out letters from a magazine," Mila said. "Why didn't she just write it?"

"Everyone's handwriting is like a fingerprint," I answered. "She didn't want to leave a clue." Then I smiled. "But everybody leaves clues. You just have to know where to look."

Mila pulled on her long black hair. "The paper is a clue," she said. "This is the same kind of paper we use for homework." The

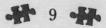

paper was grayish, with red and blue lines. Ms. Gleason made us do all our homework on the same kind of paper.

"Maybe it's from a girl in our class," I said.

"It must be," Mila said. "Or else she wouldn't have bothered to hide her handwriting."

I had liked school before this. Sure, it wasn't a cool lake on a summer day. But school was all right. Not anymore. How could I sit in a classroom knowing that some girl liked me? Wherever I went, two eyes would follow me. Yeesh. It gave me the creeps.

After taking attendance in room 201, Ms. Gleason made a special announcement. "As you know, Friday is Valentine's Day."

Everybody cheered. Valentine's Day was almost as popular as Halloween. Ms. Gleason pointed to a big box on the worktable. It was decorated with wrapping

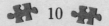

paper and hearts. "This is our post office," she said. "You have all week to bring in your valentine cards. I'll assign mail carriers to deliver the cards on Friday."

Everybody sat up straight. We all tried to look like expert mail carriers. I noticed Bigs Maloney flash a big smile at Lucy Hiller. Poor Bigs. Lucy had turned our class tough guy into a teddy bear. I looked at the other girls in room 201. Who could it be? Who had sent me the secret valentine?

"Boys, girls," Ms. Gleason said, "I know you are all very, very excited. Let me remind you how this works. There are three rules. Number one: You must send a valentine to every child in the class. Last week I gave you all a class roster to bring home to your parents. Don't forget anyone.

"Rule number two: You must do your own work. I don't want your parents filling out the cards for you."

Ralphie Jordan snapped his fingers. "Rats!"

Ms. Gleason smiled at Ralphie's joke. "Third, every card must say 'to' and 'from.' Try to be good letter writers."

During reading circle, Ms. Gleason read from a book called *Abraham Lincoln*. We had started it last week. It was a long book, so we couldn't read it all in one day. Anyway, I learned another interesting fact about Honest Abe. I wrote it down: **Abe kept**

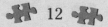

important papers in his hat! Six more facts to go.

The more I learned about Abraham Lincoln, the more I liked him. He was smart *and* strong. That's pretty good — even if he didn't play in the NBA.

At the end of school, we got our coats and hats and lined up at the door. I felt something in my pocket. Something that wasn't there this morning. It was an envelope. Inside, there were two pieces of heart candy. One said BE MINE. The other

said YOU'RE SWEET. They were both green. There was a note, too. It said:

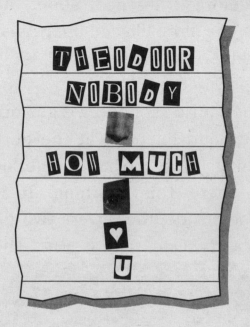

I crumpled up the note. I was going to throw it in the garbage. Then I remembered it was a clue. I had to save it. Suddenly Bobby Solofsky grabbed the note from my hand. "What are you reading, Theodore?" he said. I tried to grab it back. But Bobby handed it to his best friend, Mike Radcliffe.

"Read it, Mike," Bobby said.

Mike did. Out loud. "Jigsaw has a secret valentine," he teased. Everybody giggled. Bobby Solofsky laughed so loud I thought his head was going to fall off. I wish it had.

I hate teasers.

Chapter Three

The List of Suspects

I had time to kill before Mila came over after school. So I sat in my basement office and drank grape juice. I've had tough cases before. But this one really got under my skin.

I took out my detective journal. It was a big, fat notebook. I turned to a clean page and wrote: **SUSPECTS**. I underlined it in red. Under **SUSPECTS**, I listed all the girls in my class.

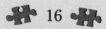

Mila Yeh   Lucy Hiller
Danika Starling   Kim Lewis
Geetha Nair   Helen Zuckerman
Athena Lorenzo   Nicole Rodriguez

I stared at the list of eight names. I took out a purple marker and crossed out Mila's name. It couldn't be Mila. She'd never do something that rotten. Besides, it was impossible. Mila was with me when the doorbell rang.

My skinny sister, Hillary, came downstairs with a load of laundry. I snapped the book closed. "What are you doing, Jigsaw?" she asked. "Writing a love poem to your new girlfriend?"

Everybody's a joker. But that's Hillary for you. She's thirteen years old. Like my brother Billy says, Hillary can't help it if she's a pain. Then I heard Rags bark. I knew Mila was here.

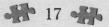

Mila was singing "The Farmer in the Dell." Except the words were different.

"It's Valentine's Day. It's Valentine's Day.
Hi-ho, what do you know!
It's Valentine's Day!"

Mila's voice was pretty. But I didn't care for the song. I told her so. "Don't be a grouch," Mila said.

I shrugged. Mila was right. This case was getting to me. "You know what the worst part is," I complained. "This girl is ruining a perfectly good holiday. I mean, I like Valentine's Day. You get to eat cupcakes. Why does she have to drag love into it?"

I showed Mila the list of suspects. She grabbed a marker and crossed out Danika Starling. "Danika gets 100s on her spelling tests." Mila explained. "Our suspect is a bad speller."

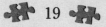

Then she crossed out Lucy Hiller. "It's not Lucy," she said.

"How do you know?" I asked.

"I think she's sweet on Bigs Maloney," Mila said.

I moved down the list. "Helen?" I asked.

"Cross it out," Mila said. "Helen is still mad about what you said about her latkes."

"They did taste like cardboard," I protested.

Mila shook her head. "How do you know? You wouldn't even *try* one."

Believe me, I knew. But I didn't argue. Mila crossed out Helen's name. There were four names left: Kim, Geetha, Athena, and Nicole. "We'd better break out my Tip-top Detective Kit," I said.

My brothers Billy, Nicholas, and Daniel chipped in and gave it to me for Christmas. It was the greatest. The kit came with a book that explained all sorts of cool things. Making fingerprints, writing secret codes, spying tips, and more. It also came with a magnifying glass, spy mirrors, rearview sunglasses, an ink pad — even an ID card.

Here's what mine looked like:

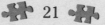

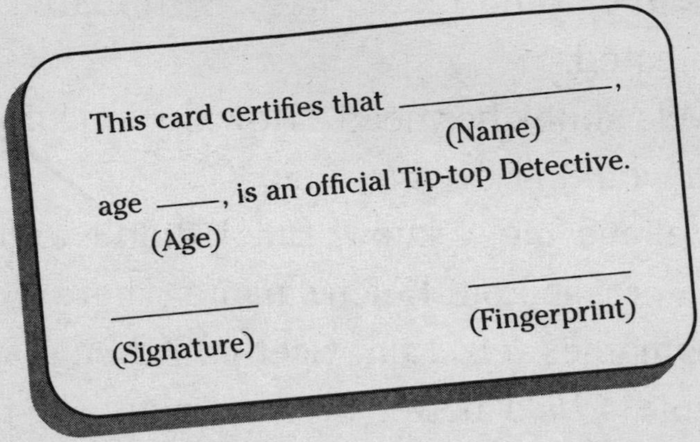

This card certifies that —————————,

(Name)

age ——, is an official Tip-top Detective.

(Age)

—————————   —————————

(Signature)   (Fingerprint)

Solving this case wasn't going to be easy. I would need every trick in the book. Fortunately, I owned the book.

And I'd read it twice.

Chapter Four
Candy Math

After dinner — and homework — I got down to business. I grabbed everything I needed and spread it on the kitchen table:

I was making a see-and-spy magazine. First I poured some globs of glue on the

inside back cover. I smushed the last page of the magazine to the back cover. Glue leaked out the edges. I should have put newspaper under the magazine. The table was getting sticky. Oh, well, too late now. The directions said to wait for the glue to dry. I counted to six. Then I cut a peephole. It wasn't very round. But that's all right. On the opposite page, I taped a small mirror.

My parents and Grams were in the living room. I sat down and pretended to read. When I held the magazine up, I could peek through the hole. To see what was happening behind me, I looked in the mirror.

Too bad nothing was happening.

But I didn't mind. My plan was set. Now I could bring it to school and spy on all four suspects. Who was sending me the notes? Was it Kim or Geetha? Athena or Nicole? Whoever it was, I wanted to catch them red-handed.

"Earth to Theodore, Earth to Theodore. Can you hear me?" My mom poked a finger through my peephole.

"MOM!" I cried. "Please, I'm NOT Theodore. I'm Jigsaw. And I'm very busy right now."

"I can see that," she said. "You're busy dripping glue all over your pants."

I looked down. White globs of glue covered my jeans. In the bathroom, my mom rinsed them off with a wet sponge. I stood in my pajamas and watched. "You know I hate it when you call me Theodore," I complained.

"It's what we named you, dear," she said.

"But no one who *likes* me calls me that," I said. "All my friends call me Jigsaw."

She kissed my forehead. "Off to bed now, Theodore. I love you — even if you don't like your name. Sleep tight." My dad came into my room and read to me, like he

 26

usually does. I fell asleep right away. It had been a long, hard day.

In school on Tuesday, Ms. Gleason gave us the best math project ever. It was delicious. No kidding! In room 201, we didn't sit in straight rows. We had clusters. I sat at a cluster with Mila, Joey Pignattano, and Geetha Nair. Ms. Gleason gave every table a plastic bag filled with candy hearts. We were supposed to work together to answer math questions. When we were done, Ms. Gleason said we could eat them.

On a worksheet called *Estimation* we had to guess how many hearts were in the bag. Joey Pignattano guessed ninety-three hearts. When we counted them, there were only forty. Then we had to subtract to find the difference.

$$\begin{array}{r} 93 \\ -40 \\ \hline 53 \end{array}$$

Joey was wrong by fifty-three hearts! We did *Classification,* too. That meant putting the candy hearts in groups by color.

"I like the pink ones best," Joey said.

"I like the purple ones," Mila said. "How about you, Geetha? Which is *your* favorite color to eat?"

Geetha shrugged. "I don't remember," she said. "I haven't eaten any since last Valentine's Day."

Mila and I looked at each other. We were

thinking the same thing: *Cross Geetha's name off the list.* My secret valentine gave me two candy hearts. Whoever it was must have saved a few hearts for herself. I was glad that it wasn't Geetha. We were just starting to be friends. It would be a shame to ruin it now.

We made candy-heart graphs. We lined up all the candy hearts by color and measured the row. We compared different kinds of candy hearts. Yellow was the

winner. We even built heart towers. Joey built his seven-hearts-high before it fell.

Finally Ms. Gleason let us eat the candy.

Math never tasted so good.

I tried out the see-and-spy magazine during recess. I watched some of the kids poking around the post office. But I didn't notice anything strange. Mike Radcliffe and Bobby Solofsky were messing around at their table. I saw it in the mirror. Bobby was trying to rip the head off a Batman action figure. What a guy.

"Let's work on Abraham Lincoln after school," Mila said to me.

"Okay," I said. "But I've got to go see Bobby Solofsky first."

Mila was surprised. She knew that Bobby Solofsky wasn't one of my best friends. "He invited me over," I explained. "Bobby said he had to talk to me. Detective to detective."

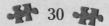

Chapter Five

A New Headache

I climbed the front steps to Bobby Solofsky's house. Thick evergreens lined the walkway. A blanket of clouds covered the sun. I rang the bell. Nothing happened. I knocked on the door. Nothing happened all over again.

Suddenly a loud scream — "YAH!" — came from behind the bushes. It nearly scared me out of my pants. I jumped off the stoop and turned around. Bobby Solofsky appeared. He pointed at me and laughed. "Ha-ha. I tricked you!"

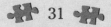 31

"Very funny," I said.

"What's the matter, Theodore?" he asked. "Are you mad because you're not the best detective in second grade anymore?"

"Oh, really?" I said. "I hadn't heard."

"Yeah," he said. "It's all over school. You can't even figure out your own secret valentine." Solofsky jerked his thumb toward the door. "Inside," he said.

I followed him into the house. "My mom's still at work," he explained. "My sister is supposed to watch me. But she's not home, either."

He sat down in a chair. I stood. "Okay, Solofsky. I'm all ears."

Bobby Solofsky slid his tongue across his teeth. Sucking sounds came from his mouth. I'd seen better manners on a farm. "Everybody knows you've got a secret valentine," he said.

"So?" I said.

 33

"So, I figure you need the help of a *real* detective," he said. "I get fifty cents a day."

"I think I'm hearing things," I said. "Did you say you want *me* to hire *you*?"

He grunted. I took that as a yes.

"Look, Solofsky," I said, "I can solve my own cases."

"You need my help," he told me. "It doesn't look good, you know. Wait until

everybody hears how Jigsaw Jones can't solve his own case."

The guy was giving me a headache. "All right, Solofsky. You're so smart. Here's a riddle for you," I said. "There's a man deep in the jungle. He's hunting tigers. It's dark and wet and there are wild animals everywhere. Suddenly he notices something in his pocket. It has a head. It has a tail. But no legs. Yet the man isn't scared. Why not?"

I watched Solofsky try to think. It looked like it hurt. He finally said, "I don't care about your stupid riddles."

"Sure," I said. I turned to leave. At the door I reached into my pocket. I flipped him a nickel. It spun head over tail. "Here you go, Solofsky," I said. "Maybe that will help you figure it out."

Chapter Six

Abe Lincoln, Mila, and Me

Mila couldn't believe it. "Bobby Solofsky said *what*?" she exclaimed.

"He said that I should hire him," I repeated.

Mila crossed her arms. "We don't need Bobby Solofsky's help."

"That's what I told him," I said. "I mean, I've got enough problems right now. I don't even want to think about Bobby Solofsky."

"Don't worry," Mila said. "No one will ever hire Bobby. Everybody knows we're the best."

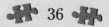 36

Mila and I were in my basement. She had come over to work on Abraham Lincoln. She looked up facts while I drew. After a while, Mila read her facts out loud.

5. Abraham Lincoln was born in a log cabin.
6. He tried to write neatly.
7. He was good at chopping wood.
8. His wife's name was Mary.
9. He freed the slaves.

"That's pretty good," I said. "Only one more fact to go. We'd better make sure it's interesting. My favorite is still the one from yesterday. *Abe kept important papers in his hat!*

I stopped drawing. "You can look now."

Mila's jaw dropped. She didn't say anything for a long time. "He's . . . he's wearing . . . shorts . . . and sneakers."

"It's a basketball uniform," I explained. "Isn't it great?"

"I don't know, Jigsaw."

"Ms. Gleason will love it," I said. "She's tall, just like Abe. Tall people are crazy about basketball."

I finished coloring in the uniform with markers. It was mostly orange and blue.

"Careful," Mila said. "You're getting messy fingerprints all over it."

Suddenly Mila got excited. I mean *real* excited. "That's it!" she screamed.

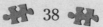

"Fingerprints! That's how we'll catch your secret admirer."

Mila and I spent the rest of the night reading about fingerprints. My detective book had a whole chapter on it. Thing is, fingerprinting seemed pretty tricky. We needed to get a sample of each suspect's fingerprints. Later on, maybe we could match them against the next valentine.

It was worth a shot.

Chapter Seven

The Fingerprint Flop

On Wednesday morning, Ms. Gleason called me up to her desk. She handed me a white envelope. "Someone left this in my mail slot," she said.

I carefully picked up the corner envelope with two fingers. I turned the envelope over. It was just like the others. My name was written with cutout letters from a magazine. "Er, thanks, Ms. Gleason."

She looked at me carefully. "Is everything all right?" she asked.

"It's a clue," I said.

"Of course, a clue," Ms. Gleason said. "Silly me. Would you like to put that in a plastic bag?" Ms. Gleason reached into her desk drawer. She leaned forward and whispered, "I think that's how the police do it on television."

"Really? Sure, thanks," I said.

Ms. Gleason opened a bag. I dropped the envelope inside. She zipped it closed and handed it to me. "You'd make a pretty good detective," I told her. "Too bad you're a teacher."

I was eager to read the note. But after last time, I decided to wait until no one was around. Going back to my desk, I peeked at Nicole and Athena. They weren't paying any attention to me.

"Where's Kim?" I whispered to Mila.

"She's home sick," Mila said.

I showed her the bag. "This came today."

"That leaves two," Mila said. "Only Athena and Nicole are left."

Athena or Nicole. Athena had big eyes that bulged out like a goldfish's. Nicole had a rabbit nose. It twitched a lot. One of them loved me. I hoped it wouldn't last forever. But whoever it was, she was faking it pretty well. All during class, I watched both suspects closely. I watched what they did. I watched what they touched — *especially* what they touched.

I got my chance during gym class. It was risky. But I had to try it. When everybody

got in line, I hid behind the bookcase. It was a good spot. No one missed me. I heard feet clomp into the hallway. Ms. Gleason flicked off the light and shut the door.

I was alone.

In a dark room.

I had to work fast. I flipped on the light and checked the hallway. No one there. I quickly got my fingerprinting kit together: tape, a magnifying glass, a small paintbrush, black construction paper, and baby powder. I went to Athena's work area first. I tried to sprinkle a tiny bit of baby powder on it. But something was stuck. I gave the powder another squeeze. A huge pile squirted out. A puff of dust rose like a cloud. I coughed for a long time.

Then — very, very softly — I brushed the powder until it was a thin layer of dust. Fingerprints were supposed to appear. They didn't. So I tried another spot.

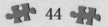

Then another. Pouring powder, brushing it, searching for prints. It got kind of messy.

Finally, I found a smudge. I laid a piece of tape over it, then yanked the tape up fast. I put the tape on the black paper. A print was supposed to appear. Like magic. It looked like a blob of baby powder to me. But I didn't give up. I just kept pouring baby powder all over the place.

I didn't even hear the door open.

Maybe I lost track of the time. Maybe Ms. Gleason came back early. All I heard was my name. "THEODORE!" Ms. Gleason didn't use her inside voice. No, it was her outside voice, that's for sure. I'll say this for Ms. Gleason: She's got good lungs.

Chapter Eight
The Class Rules

Ms. Gleason calmed down after a while. And then she was really nice about everything.

I mean really, really, really nice.

She even apologized for yelling. I told her I was sorry, too. We cleaned up the mess together. And we talked. She seemed worried about me. Go figure. Best of all, no one else found out. It was our secret.

Sure, Ms. Gleason gave me extra

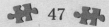

homework. She handed me a copy of the class rules. I had to write them over neatly — like Abraham Lincoln. "I want you to think about what you did, Theodore," she told me. "I want you to think about why it was wrong. Think about why it's dangerous when people don't follow the rules."

I figure I got off easy. Here are the rules:

1. Listen when others are speaking.
2. Keep our classroom neat.
3. Be polite.
4. Keep hands and feet to yourself.
5. Use quiet, inside voices.
6. Be kind to others.
7. Work together.
8. Walk in the halls and the classroom.
9. Respect other people's things.
10. Be responsible.

After dinner, I went into my room and worked on a jigsaw puzzle. It was called Birds of Florida. The puzzle was in the shape of a circle. That made it harder to do the edges. But puzzles are like mysteries. You just have to keep putting the pieces together. One at a time.

I pulled out the day's note.

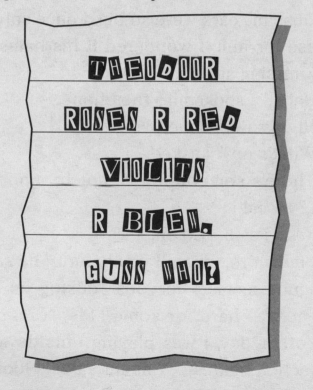

THEODOOR
ROSES R RED
VIOLITS
R BLEU.
GUSS WHO?

Now I had three notes. I laid them on my bed, side by side. I stared at them for a long time. Then my brother Billy poked his head into the room. "Somebody's on the phone for you, Jigsaw. I think it's Wingnut."

"Wingnut?" I said, surprised. Wingnut O'Brien was my next-door neighbor. He was six. Everyone called him Wingnut because his ears were so big. I once solved a case for him. I wondered if his hamster was missing again.

"Hello," I spoke into the phone.

"Hi, Jigsaw. It's me, Wingnut."

"What's up?" I asked.

"There's something I've got to, um, tell you," he said.

"Yes," I said. "Go on."

"I meant to, um, tell you before," he said. Wingnut seemed nervous. Talking on the phone was hard for some kids. "Um, see, the other day, I was playing outside with my action figures," Wingnut said. "I looked

 50

up and saw a girl, um, ring your doorbell and run away."

I closed my eyes. "When?"

"Um, let's see," Wingnut said. "Sunday. At two-thirty."

That sounded about right. "Did you see who it was?" I asked.

Wingnut paused. "Um, hold on." He put down the phone. He was back after a few seconds. "Um, yeah. It was that friend of yours. The basketball player."

"Do you mean Danika?" I asked.

"Yeah," Wingnut said. "That's her. Danika. Um, can I go now? My, um, mom says I can't talk on the phone too much."

"Sure, Wingnut. And thanks," I said. "Thanks a lot."

I hung up the phone and went back to my room. Something wasn't right. Danika was the best speller in our class. Could she have spelled words wrong — *on purpose*?

That didn't sound like Danika Starling to me. She liked to do things right.

I pulled out my detective journal. I jotted down what Wingnut told me.

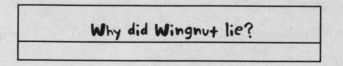

Wingnut.

Playing with superheroes.

Saw Danika.

2:30.

Alone?

Then I added a final line:

Why did Wingnut lie?

Chapter Nine

Honest Jones

Thursday morning I told Mila about Wingnut's phone call.

"I'm surprised," Mila said. "Wingnut has treated you like a superhero ever since we found his hamster. What makes you think he was lying?"

"Wait a minute," I said. "Did you say *superhero*?"

Mila made a face. "Yeah. So?"

"You just gave me an idea," I said. "Look, we've got a lot to do." I asked Mila to talk

to Danika. "Try to find out where she was on Sunday afternoon. We'll deal with Wingnut after school," I said.

We had another good day in class. In art, we made our own mailboxes for the Valentine's Day party. We would keep them on our tables for the mail carriers. Ms. Gleason picked three names from a hat. The winners got to deliver the cards the next day. She picked Ralphie, Bigs, and Mila. They were really happy about it. All the while, I watched Athena and Nicole. But they didn't seem to notice I was alive. That was a relief.

Besides, I was beginning to suspect someone else.

Ms. Gleason read poems to us during reading circle. She took out a book called *Valentine's Day Stories and Poems.* The poems were pretty funny. We were all getting into the holiday spirit. After reading

circle, Ms. Gleason gave us time to write our own poems. Almost everybody wrote about Valentine's Day. Poems about hearts and hugs and cards and kisses. Yeesh. I wrote mine about Abraham Lincoln. But I'm still not sure if "Lincoln" and "thinking" make a rhyme.

I read it to Ms. Gleason:

Abraham Lincoln was always thinking.
He was skinny. Not fat.
He kept papers in his hat!

Ms. Gleason loved it! She told me that I was a poet. I promised her that from now on, I was going to be like Honest Abe. "No more tricky stuff," I said. "Just call me Honest Jones."

Mila hung around with Danika during recess. She pulled me aside later on. "Get this," Mila said. "Danika went roller-skating on Sunday afternoon."

"Any witnesses?" I asked.

"Yes, she was with Lucy and Kim."

"Then I was right," I said. "Wingnut lied."

Mila and I sat together on the bus ride home. We always do. But I didn't talk much. I just stared out the window, watching the houses slide past. I thought about Wingnut O'Brien.

"You still haven't told me," Mila said. "How did you know Wingnut was lying?"

"I didn't know for sure," I said. "But something in his story was fishy. What I couldn't figure out was *why*."

I continued. "Something about this case has been wrong from the beginning. It's like we are doing a puzzle. We put all the facts together — but there is still a big piece missing."

"Tell me," Mila said. "What's the missing piece?"

"That's what we're trying to find out," I answered.

Chapter Ten
To Catch a Lie

Wingnut's teenage brother, Jake the Snake, answered the door.

"You!" he said. Jake took a step back. I made Jake nervous. That's because I once threw up on his Air Jordans. He's never forgiven me. "What do you and your friend want, Sherlock?" he said.

I stared at Jake. He wore black sneakers, black jeans, and a Megadeath T-shirt. His pet boa constrictor, Goliath, was nowhere in sight. "Your hair," I said. "It's green."

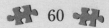

Jake sneered. He was a real joy to be around. Yeesh.

"Is Wingnut home?" Mila asked.

Jake groaned and walked away. He left the door wide open. I guess that was his way of saying, "Please follow me." So we did. Jake rapped on Wingnut's door. "Hey, worm," he called. "Sherlock Holmes and Dr. Watson are here." Jake went into his room across the hall and slammed the door.

Wingnut came to the door. "Hi, Jigsaw. Hi, Mila. What are you guys doing here?"

Wingnut was wearing the usual. Jeans and a hockey jersey. He'd just gotten a haircut. It made his ears look bigger than ever. If that was possible.

"We need to ask you some questions," Mila said.

"Um, ah, sure," he said. "Come on in."

"Mind if we go outside?" Mila asked. "I'm allergic to hamster fur, remember?"

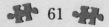

We headed out the door. It was another cold, gray day. I told Wingnut to show us where he was playing when he saw Danika.

Wingnut led us to the end of his driveway. "I was right here."

I checked my journal. "Alone?" I asked.

Wingnut nodded and looked away.

"Tell us what happened," Mila said. "Nice and slow."

Wingnut pulled on his ear. He said to me, "I already told you everything I know."

"I don't think so," I replied.

Wingnut pulled on his ear again. He looked at the ground. He looked at the cloudy sky. He looked everywhere — except into my eyes. Slowly, carefully, he told his tale all over again. He was playing alone. It was 2:30. He saw Danika Starling go to my house, ring the bell, and run away.

"That's very strange," I said. "I don't see any clocks around here. Do you, Mila?"

Wingnut scratched the back of his neck.

 62

"You must have been wearing a watch, right, Wingnut?" I offered.

Wingnut scratched again.

I took a step closer. "Do you have fleas?" I asked. "All that scratching. It makes me think you're either very itchy . . . or you're not telling the truth."

Wingnut looked at the ground. I think he was looking for a rock to crawl under. It was now or never. So I took my best guess. "Someone made you lie, right?"

Bull's-eye.

Wingnut looked up, surprised. He didn't say yes. He didn't say no. But he didn't have to say anything. The answer was in his eyes.

"You don't even own a watch," I said. "Right?"

"Right," Wingnut whispered. "I don't tell time so good."

"Let me ask you something," I said. "You still have that great action figure

collection? You've got Spider-Man, the Hulk, Superman — all those guys, right?"

Wingnut nodded happily. "Yes, and I have Hawkman and Batman and —"

"Let me see Batman," I interrupted.

That was the zinger. Wingnut looked at Mila. He wasn't smiling anymore. He looked like he might cry. The poor guy loved his superheroes, all right. He loved them so much he'd even lie for them.

"Look, Wingnut," I said. "I've got a pretty good idea what happened. I know you don't want to lie. Deep down, you're a good guy. You're just like Honest Abe Lincoln. But somebody made you lie, right?"

"Yeah," Wingnut confessed in a soft voice.

"You don't have to say any more," I told him. "It wasn't your fault." We turned to leave. After two steps, I stopped. "One more thing, Wingnut," I said. "Don't worry. We'll get your Batman back."

A big smile crossed his face.

And for the first time all week, the sun fought its way through the clouds. Things looked better already.

Chapter Eleven
The Trap Is Set

Mila and I sat in my office. We each ate a cookie and had a glass of grape juice. "That was our big mistake," I said. "We figured the notes were sent because someone *liked* me. But they were sent because someone *didn't* like me.

"The clues were there all the time," I explained. I ticked them off on my fingers. "The notes were written to Theodore. Bobby Solofsky is the only kid in our class

who calls me Theodore — and he does that just to bug me.

"Number two," I said. "Bobby just started his own detective business. But nobody would hire him. He wanted to make me look bad. He figured then he might be able to take my cases."

"*Our* cases," Mila corrected.

"Anyway, he figured wrong," I said. "But

making Wingnut lie was his big mistake. The thing is, I saw Bobby with a Batman toy a few days ago. But I didn't think anything of it."

Mila snapped her fingers. "That's how he got Wingnut to lie. Bobby Solofsky stole his Batman!"

"Pretty rotten," I said. "I figure Wingnut did see somebody ring and run on Sunday. But it wasn't Danika. It was Bobby."

"So Bobby takes Batman," Mila said, "and says he won't give it back unless Wingnut keeps quiet."

"Right," I said. "Then maybe Bobby tries to get clever. He tells Wingnut to call me up with a phony clue."

Mila just shook her head.

We sat in silence for a long time. We wanted to get back at Bobby Solofsky. Finally we came up with the perfect plan. It took a few phone calls to set the trap. We

69

asked a few favors. First we called Bigs Maloney. Then Ralphie Jordan. Along with Mila, they were delivering the valentine cards tomorrow. They agreed to help us.

I suddenly banged my forehead. "Oh, no!" I shouted. "I forgot to do my valentine cards. Yeesh!"

Mila left as I was begging Mom to drive me to the Party Store. My mom sighed. She groaned. She made a fuss. But I knew she'd take me. I needed a set of valentine cards. I *had* to have them.

In the car, my mom asked me what song I was singing. "Oh, it's one of Mila's," I said. In a few minutes, we were both singing it together:

"It's Valentine's Day. It's Valentine's Day.
Hi-ho, what do you know!
It's Valentine's Day!"

Chapter Twelve

Happy Valentine's Day

.

First thing Friday morning, Mila and I gave Ms. Gleason our Abraham Lincoln project. I was right. Ms. Gleason thought it was funny to see Abe in a basketball uniform. At the last minute, I added a basketball to the picture. Ms. Gleason said we were very creative.

Mila handed Ms. Gleason the list of facts. "Read it," Mila said. "Jigsaw wrote number ten all by himself."

We couldn't wait for her to finish reading.

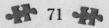

"Very nice job, you two," Ms. Gleason said. "I guess I learn something new every day." We laughed. Fact number ten was sort of a joke. It read, *Abraham Lincoln was tall enough to dunk a basketball.*

We took our seats. Before the pledge, Ms. Gleason said, "Excuse me, Theodore. You know the rule. No hats in the classroom."

I stood up for everyone to see. "But Ms. Gleason," I said, "that's where I keep my important papers!" I pulled off my baseball cap — and all my valentine cards tumbled out.

Everybody laughed.

Bigs, Ralphie, and Mila delivered the cards right before lunch. One by one, they dropped cards into everybody's mailbox. Everybody's except for Bobby Solofsky's. As everyone got more cards, the class became more and more excited. The room was filled with whoops and shouts and happy voices.

"Did you get mine?"

"Wow, thanks!"

"All right — another Garfield!"

"Thanks, everybody!"

I watched Bobby Solofsky. He kept waiting for cards to be delivered. But nothing came. He slumped lower and lower in his chair. He finally rested his chin on the table. Bobby Solofsky looked pretty bummed out.

I walked up to him and tossed an envelope onto his desk. It had his name on it — in cutout letters from a magazine. Bobby Solofsky looked at me and swallowed hard.

"Open it," I said.

Bobby couldn't read the message. That's because it looked like this:

14-9-3-5 20-18-25,

2-21-20 9 1-13

19-20-9-12-12 20-8-5 2-5-19-20!

"It's a substitution code," I explained. "Each number stands for a letter in the alphabet. Number one is letter A. Number two is letter B. Number three is letter C. Get it?"

While Bobby tried to figure out the message, I walked over to his cubby. I grabbed the Batman action figure. "Hey!" he said.

"Hey nothing," I told him. "I'm giving this back to Wingnut O'Brien."

Bobby didn't say a word. He was caught and he knew it.

Just then, Mila, Bigs, and Ralphie came over. They dumped a big pile of valentine cards onto Bobby's desk. "We tricked you," they cried. "Happy Valentine's Day!"

Even Bobby Solofsky had to smile. He appreciated a good trick.